NICHOLAS HELLER

Mathilda the Dream Bear

GREENWILLOW BOOKS New York

for Annabeth

Watercolor and acrylic paints and a black
pen were used for the full-color art.
The text type is Egyptian 505.

Printed in Singapore by Tien Wah Press
First Edition
10 9 8 7 6 5 4 3 2 1

Library of Congress Cataloging-in-Publication Data

Heller, Nicholas
Mathilda the dream bear.
Summary: With the wave of her wand,
Mathilda the Dream Bear brings slumbering
animals very pleasant dreams.
[1. Dreams—Fiction.   2. Sleep—Fiction.
3. Animals—Fiction]   I. Title.
PZ7.H37426Mat 1989   [E]   88-4830
ISBN 0-688-08238-6
ISBN 0-688-08239-4 (lib. bdg.)

The dog was asleep.

And the cats were asleep.

The fish were asleep.

And the bird was almost asleep

when in through
the keyhole
flew Mathilda
the Dream Bear.

She landed silently on the carpet, took off
her mittens and boots, and set off on tiptoe
across the living room.

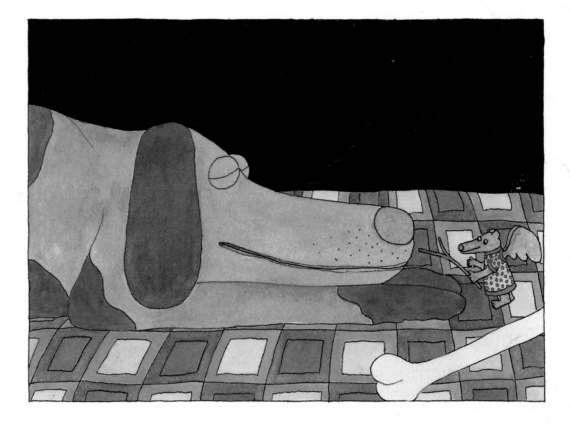

Soon she came to the dog.

"Hello, Dog," she whispered. "I have a fine dream for you tonight." And she waved her wand underneath the dog's nose.

Suddenly the dog began to dream.

He was the guest of honor at a huge banquet,
and all the neighborhood dogs were there.

And all the neighborhood cats, in jackets and bow ties, were running back and forth from the kitchen, bringing them roasts and stews and steaks and chops.

And as the dog dreamed of eating and eating
as much as he wanted, Mathilda flew across
the room to where the cats were sleeping.

"Good evening, Cats," Mathilda whispered.
"I have a dream for you, too." And she brushed
her wand gently against their whiskers.

The cats began to dream.

They were the lead dancers in a ballet.

They leapt and pirouetted,

and the audience applauded.

Mathilda flew over to the fish tank.

She tapped her wand softly on the glass,

and the fish began to dream, too.

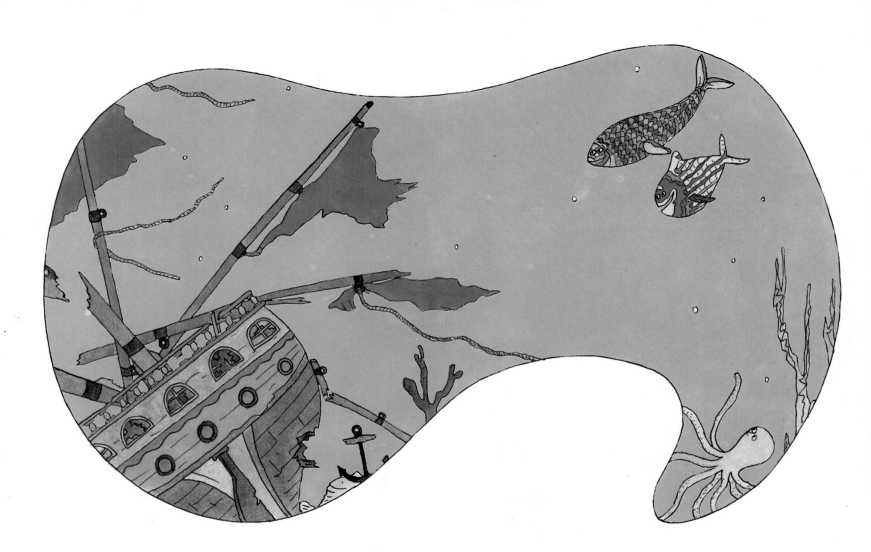

They were swimming along the bottom of
the ocean, and they saw a sunken ship.

They swam through one of the portholes, and there was a mermaid with a harp playing beautiful music.

As the fish listened to the mermaid,

Mathilda quietly put on her mittens and boots,

and was just about to fly through the
keyhole when she heard a loud whisper.
"Hey."

It was the bird.

"What about me?" he said. "Don't I get a dream?"

"I'm sorry," said Mathilda. "I didn't see you up there on your perch. Of course I have a dream for you—we can even have one together. I need some sleep, too."

So Mathilda lay down on the perch. After a while they dozed off, and this is what they dreamed.

They were flying through the moonlit night,

higher and higher above the earth,

until they were flying in outer space,
higher than anyone had been before.

Just before dawn, Mathilda woke up.

She slipped quietly off the perch, and leaving

the animals to finish their dreams,

she vanished through the keyhole.

D